KU-799-087

Miranda Finds a Bell

by

Lucy Kincaid

Illustrated by Tom Hirst

BRIMAX · NEWMARKET · ENGLAND

Miranda Goose is always dreaming.
She dreams when she is asleep.
She dreams when she is awake.
She walks with her head in the air.
She forgets to look where she is
going.

Miranda doesn't see the ducks.
She almost steps on them.
The ducks jump out of her way.
The ducks bump into each other.
"Quack! Quack!" say the ducks.
The ducks are angry.
"I'm sorry," says Miranda.
Miranda does not see the cat.
She steps on the cat's tail.
"Meow!" says the cat.
The cat is angry.
"I'm sorry," says Miranda.

Miranda has her head in the air. She is not looking where she is going. She does not see the meeting. She walks into the middle of it. What a mess!

"How did that happen?" asks Miranda.

"You weren't looking where you were going," says the dog.

"I'm sorry," says Miranda.

"I will try not to do it again."

Miranda does try. She tries very hard.
But she still walks with her head in the air.
No one is safe. Everyone jumps out of her way when they can. But sometimes they are busy. They do not see her coming.

Miranda has her head in the air.
She sees a bell on a ribbon.
It is caught in a bush.
"I have found some treasure," says
Miranda.
She pushes her head through the
loop of the ribbon. The bell hangs
round her neck like a necklace.

Ting-a-ling! Ting-a-ling!
"What is that noise?" say the hens.
"It's Miranda," say the ducks.
"We can hear her coming," says the cat.
"We can get out of her way before she bumps into us," says the dog.